Emily
the Emerald
Fairy

by Daisy Meadows

illustrated by Georgie Ripper

Join the Rainbow Magic Reading Challenge!

Read the story and collect your fairy points to climb the Reading Rainbow online. Turn to the back of the book for details!

This book is worth 5 points.

The Jewel Fairies

To Annabelle Argent – with love
and fairy magic!

Special thanks to
Narinder Dhami

ORCHARD BOOKS

First published in Great Britain in 2005 by Orchard Books
This edition published in 2016 by The Watts Publishing Group

3 5 7 9 10 8 6 4 2

© 2016 Rainbow Magic Limited.
© 2016 HIT Entertainment Limited.
Illustrations © Georgie Ripper 2005

HiT entertainment

A CIP catalogue record for this book is available from the British Library.

ISBN 978 1 40834 874 1

Printed and bound by CPI Group (UK) Ltd, Croydon, CR0 4YY

MIX
Paper from
responsible sources
FSC® C104740

The paper and board used in this book are made from wood from responsible sources

Orchard Books
An imprint of Hachette Children's Group
Part of The Watts Publishing Group Limited
Carmelite House, 50 Victoria Embankment, London EC4Y 0DZ

An Hachette UK Company
www.hachette.co.uk
www.hachettechildrens.co.uk

By Frosty magic I cast away
These seven jewels with their fiery rays,
So their magic powers will not be felt
And my icy castle shall not melt.

The fairies may search high and low
To find the gems and take them home.
But I will send my goblin guards
To make the fairies' mission hard.

Contents

Toy Trouble

"Wow!" Kirsty Tate gasped, her
eyes wide with amazement. "This is
the biggest toy shop I've ever seen!"

Her best friend, Rachel Walker,
laughed. "I know," she agreed.
"It's brilliant, isn't it?"

Kirsty nodded. Wherever she turned,
there was something wonderful to see.

In one corner of the toy shop was an enormous display of dolls in every shape and size, together with a spectacular array of dolls' houses.
A special, roped-off area was filled with remote-control cars, buses, lorries and aeroplanes, and nearby stood rows of bikes, trikes and silver scooters.

Shelves were piled high with every single board game Kirsty had ever heard of, stacks of electronic games and a variety of computer consoles. Colourful kites hung from the ceiling, along with multi-coloured balloons and marvellous mobiles. Kirsty had never seen anything like it, and this was only the ground floor!

"Look over there, Kirsty," Rachel said, pointing at the dolls.

Kirsty saw a sign saying, *Meet Fairy Florence and her friends.* She stared at the dolls grouped around the sign. Fairy Florence wore a long pink dress, and looked rather dull and old-fashioned. Kirsty and Rachel glanced at each other and burst out laughing.

"Fairy Florence doesn't look anything like a real fairy!" Rachel whispered, and Kirsty nodded.

Rachel and Kirsty knew what real fairies looked like because they'd met them, many times. The two girls had often visited Fairyland to help their friends when they were in trouble. The cause of the problem was usually cold, spiky Jack Frost, who was always making mischief with the help of his mean goblin servants.

Just a few days ago, King Oberon and Queen Titania had called on Rachel and Kirsty to help them, after Jack Frost had stolen the seven magic gems from the Queen's tiara. The seven jewels were very important because they controlled much of the magic in Fairyland.

Jack Frost had wanted the magic for himself, but after the heat and light of the jewels began to melt his ice castle, he had angrily cast the gems out into the human world. Now it was up to the girls to find the jewels and return them to Fairyland, before the fairies' magic ran out.

"I hope we find the rest of the magic jewels before I go home," Kirsty said to Rachel, looking a bit worried. "After all, I'm only staying with you till the end of half-term."

"Well, we've found India's Moonstone and Scarlett's Garnet," Rachel reminded her. "We've just got to keep our eyes open."

"Yes, for goblins, as well as magic jewels!" Kirsty pointed out. The girls knew that Jack Frost had sent his goblin servants to find and guard the gems, to stop the fairies from getting them back.

"Ah, here you are, girls," said Mr Walker, Rachel's dad, as he joined them. "Do you two want to look around on your own? We can meet up later."

"Dad can't wait to get to the train section," Rachel told Kirsty with a grin. "It's his favourite bit."

Mr Walker laughed. "Ah, but today I have the perfect excuse," he said. "I'm buying something for my godson,

Mark. It's his birthday soon, and he's mad about trains."

Toot, toot!

The sudden sound of a whistle made Kirsty jump.

"Look out, Kirsty," Rachel cried, with a smile. "There's a train coming!"

Kirsty looked up. For the first time she noticed that a train track ran all around the shop above their heads, weaving its way in and out of the displays.

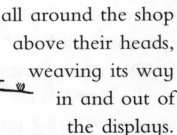

A toy train was whizzing along the track towards them, blowing its whistle.

"Fantastic, isn't it?" Mr Walker said, beaming as the train sped past. "I'll see you two later. Meet me at the shop entrance in half an hour."

"OK," Rachel replied. She grinned at Kirsty. "Come on, let's have a look around."

The girls walked off across the shop. They wandered past the dolls, and over to the roped-off area where customers were playing with remote-control cars.

"Aren't they fast?" Kirsty remarked, staring at a bright red, shiny car which was zooming up and down the floor.

"I think we should buy this red one."
The woman standing beside Kirsty said,
turning to her husband with a smile.
"Stuart will love it!"

Her husband, who was operating the
control, pushed a button. The car skidded
to a halt, then flipped right over and
landed on its wheels again, before
zooming off.

"That's great!" Kirsty gasped, looking very impressed.

"Isn't it?" the woman agreed, giving the two girls a friendly smile. "Our little boy, Stuart, will really enjoy playing with it." She glanced at her husband, who was now making the car whizz round in circles. "If he gets a chance, that is!"

Rachel and Kirsty laughed. They were just turning to move away when, suddenly, Kirsty blinked. She had caught sight of something out of the corner of her eye: something silvery and glittering...

Kirsty spun round. There was a long mirror on the wall near her, and the surface of the glass was moving – rippling and shimmering, just like a pool of clear water.

"Oh!" Kirsty gasped. "Rachel, look!"

Rachel stared at the shimmering surface of the mirror, and her eyes widened. "Is it magic?" she whispered.

As the girls watched in amazement, a reflection appeared in the shimmering glass.

Rachel and Kirsty could see a small boy, about seven years old, playing with the same shiny, red car the girls had seen a minute earlier. Smiling as he watched the toy, the boy pushed the joystick on the remote control. The little red car came whizzing straight towards the girls.

Rachel and Kirsty turned round quickly, ready to jump out of the way of the speeding car. But to their astonishment, there was nothing there. The boy and his toy car had vanished!

Both Kirsty and Rachel blinked hard, and
stared around the shop. There were other
little boys, but they couldn't see the boy
they had been watching in the mirror.
How could he have disappeared so
quickly?

"What happened?" Rachel asked,
rubbing her eyes. "Were we seeing things?"

Kirsty turned back to the mirror
again. The magical shimmer had gone
from the glass now, and it looked
completely flat and normal again. In
the mirror, Kirsty saw the man and
his wife who had been looking at the
red car, now paying for the toy at
the counter.

"But the boy looked real," she said to Rachel in a puzzled voice.

"It must be fairy magic," Rachel whispered, as they walked off. "But what does it mean?"

"I don't know," Kirsty replied. "Maybe we'll find out soon!"

The girls walked into another part of the shop which sold jokes and pocket-money toys. There were shelves full of rubbery fake spiders, plastic soldiers, dinosaurs and farm animals, as well as pencils, erasers, paints and beads.

"Mum!" A little girl was running down the aisle towards Rachel and Kirsty. She looked very excited, and

 was waving a large, plastic bottle of bubble mixture in her hand. "Mum, where are you? I want this one! It says it blows the biggest bubbles in the world!"

But just as the little girl passed Rachel and Kirsty, the bottle slipped from her fingers. It crashed to the floor and cracked open. Frothy bubble liquid spilled out all over the white shop floor.

"Oh!" the little girl gasped, and burst into tears.

"Don't cry," Kirsty said quickly. "It was just an accident."

Just then, the little girl's mum hurried towards them, followed by one of the shop assistants.

"Oh, Katie!" her mum said, giving her daughter a hug. "Don't worry, I'll buy you another one just the same."

"And we'll get that cleaned up right away," said the shop assistant kindly.

"Thank you," Katie's mum said gratefully.

Smiling now, the little girl and her mum walked off to find another bottle of bubble mixture, while the shop assistant went to get a mop.

"Shall we go and look at the dolls' houses?" Kirsty suggested.

But Rachel was staring at the floor in amazement. "Kirsty, look at that!" she whispered, clutching her friend's arm.

Kirsty looked down. The pool of spilt bubble mixture was shimmering and rippling, just like the mirror! Slowly, the girls saw a picture begin to form in the liquid. It was Katie. She seemed to be playing happily in a sunny garden, blowing beautiful, big bubbles.

"This has to be fairy magic," Rachel said as the picture faded. "I think we're seeing things that are going to happen in the future! We saw Katie playing with her bubbles at home, and the little boy with the red car must have been Stuart."

Kirsty looked thoughtful. "Do you think the magic Emerald could be somewhere nearby?" she asked. "After all, that controls seeing magic."

Rachel nodded. "I think you're right—" she began.

Toot, toot!

The girls glanced up to see the shop's little train, chugging along its track, just above their heads.

But as it came closer, Rachel stared. "There's something sparkly in the engine cab," she pointed out.

Kirsty peered hard at the engine and suddenly realised what Rachel had seen. "It's Emily the Emerald Fairy!" she gasped happily.

A Goblin Drops In

Emily was leaning out of the train and waving her sparkly, emerald-green wand at Rachel and Kirsty. As the train drew level with the girls, Emily fluttered out and flew down to land on Rachel's shoulder. She wore a short emerald-green dress and ballet slippers in exactly the same shade of green.

Long, straight, shiny red hair tumbled down her back, held off her face by a dazzling emerald clip in the shape of a dragonfly.

"At last!" Emily beamed, her green eyes sparkling. "I'm so glad to see you. I've been looking for you everywhere!"

"And we're glad to see you," Kirsty replied. "Some really strange things have been happening."

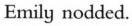

"Let's get out of sight behind that display rack," said Rachel quickly, looking round to make sure nobody was watching them. "We've got lots to tell you, Emily!"

When they were safely hidden from the other customers, the girls explained about the pictures they'd seen in the mirror and the bubble mixture.

Emily nodded. "That's seeing magic," she told them. "It means my Emerald is somewhere close by."

"We'll help you look for it," said Kirsty.

"But there are lots of places it could be," Rachel added, frowning as she looked around the enormous shop.

"And there are lots of places for goblins to hide too," Emily pointed out. She fluttered down and slipped into Rachel's pocket. "We must be careful."

The two girls walked into the middle of the shop and began to wander through the displays. Emily peeped out of Rachel's pocket.

Suddenly, Rachel grabbed Kirsty's arm. "What's that green sparkle?" she said excitedly.

"Where?" Kirsty asked.

"Over there, in the doll section," Rachel replied. Her heart beating very fast, she led the way across the room to the glimmer of green she had seen in the distance. "I know it's around here somewhere…"

"Was it that?" Kirsty asked, pointing at one of the dolls that was wearing a necklace of shiny green beads, which glittered in the light.

Rachel peered at it more closely, and her face fell. "Yes, I think it was," she sighed.

"Don't worry," whispered Emily, popping her head out of Rachel's pocket. "I'm sure we'll find it if we keep looking."

The girls walked around the shop, searching amongst the toys, but they didn't see any sign of the magic Emerald.

"There's a green glow over there!" said Emily, suddenly.

"What is it?" The girls rushed over to look. But they were disappointed to find that the green light was coming from a computer game.

"I really don't think the Emerald is anywhere down here," said Rachel, shaking her head.

Kirsty glanced upwards. "What about the floor above?" she suggested.

The girls and Emily took the lift up to the next floor. It was much quieter here. There were hardly any customers around, and the only shop assistant was busy with some paperwork behind the till.

"My Emerald must be here somewhere," Emily whispered, as they walked out of the lift. "It's not far away; I can feel it!"

Kirsty blinked. Was that a green
sparkle she'd just seen, or was she
imagining it? No, there it was again.
"I see something!" she said excitedly.
"Over there, in the cuddly toy section."

The girls and Emily hurried over to
take a closer look. There were hundreds
of plush cuddly toys, including lots of
teddy bears and almost every animal
under the sun. Rachel and Kirsty gazed

around at the cuddly cats, dogs, cows, penguins, zebras and other creatures. There was even a big golden lion, with a shaggy, bronze mane.

"Look," Kirsty said, pointing at a furry black cat. It sat at the very top of a pyramid of soft toys, and it had long, silky fur. But Rachel saw that it also had almond-shaped, green eyes that glittered and glowed in the light.

"Could one of the cat's eyes be your Emerald, Emily?" asked Rachel, staring up at the toy.

"Let me see," Emily replied. She fluttered out of Rachel's pocket, and flew up to the cat, looking closely at its eyes. After a moment, she let out a tiny scream of delight, and pointed to the cat's right eye. "This is my Emerald!" she cried.

Kirsty and Rachel beamed at each other.

"Kirsty, could you get the cat down, please?" Emily called. "It's too heavy for me to lift."

Kirsty nodded and stretched up
towards the cat. If she stood
on tiptoe, she thought
she would just be
able to reach.

Vrrrrooooom!
Kirsty glanced
up as she heard
the growl of an
engine overhead.
As she did so,
she saw that
Rachel and Emily
were also looking
for the source of
the noise.

Suddenly, the girls
spotted a large, silver toy
plane flying straight towards them.

The pilot wore flying goggles, gloves and a long, white scarf. But as Kirsty stared, she saw that his skin was green; one of Jack Frost's goblins was manning the controls!

Kirsty turned back to the magic Emerald, determined to pick it up before the goblin arrived. But, just as she stretched out her hand to grab the toy cat, the plane swooped towards her. As the plane zoomed past, the goblin reached out with one gloved hand and snatched the cat right out of Kirsty's fingers!

Goblin Getaway

"Ha ha ha!" the goblin cackled gleefully.
"The magic Emerald is mine!"

"Come back!" Emily shouted, as
Kirsty and Rachel stared at each other
in dismay. "Give me back my Emerald!"

The goblin poked his tongue out at her.
"You can't catch me!" he sneered, and bent
over the controls. The plane began to turn.

"He's getting away!" Rachel gasped.
Bravely, Emily flew up to the plane
and tried to pull the cat out of the
goblin's grasp. But
he let go of the
plane's controls for a
moment and gave
her a nasty shove.
The plane dipped
and swerved, but
the goblin soon
regained control.
Meanwhile, poor
Emily had been
sent tumbling through
the air, her wings flapping
wildly as she tried to recover her
balance. Luckily, she landed gently in
the pyramid of soft toys.

Rachel turned to Kirsty. "Quick!" she cried. "You go and make sure Emily is OK, while I try to stop the goblin from getting away."

Kirsty nodded. "Emily," she called anxiously, as she rushed to help the little fairy. "Are you all right?"

"I'm fine!" Emily panted, struggling to her feet on the trunk of a cuddly pink elephant. "But please don't let that goblin escape with my Emerald!"

Rachel was looking desperately around for a way to stop the goblin in his tracks. His plane was heading towards the lift, and if he made it into the elevator, Rachel thought they might never get the Emerald back.

Suddenly, she spied a huge bunch of helium balloons tied to one of the displays in the goblin's path. She raced over and untied the knot as quickly as she could. Just as the goblin flew overhead, Rachel released the balloons. They immediately soared upwards, surrounding the plane on all sides.

"Hey, what's going on?" Rachel heard the goblin splutter. "I can't see anything!" Rachel looked up. The goblin was trying to bat the balloons away, but to do that he was forced to let go of the controls. The plane dipped forwards, and nose-dived.

"Help!" the goblin roared. He dropped the toy cat and covered his eyes with both hands. "I'm going to crash!"

The plane and the black cat both crash-landed in a pile of teddy bears, and disappeared beneath them.

Rachel, Kirsty and Emily rushed over, as the goblin began to climb out of the heap of toys, muttering crossly under his breath.

"He's dropped the Emerald," Emily whispered to the girls. "Let's find it and get out of here."

Kirsty and Rachel began searching through the pile of teddies. The goblin glared at them and then dived into the heap of toys himself, throwing teddies here and there as he burrowed out of sight.

"We must find the Emerald before he does," urged Kirsty.

"Too late!" The goblin declared nastily, as he crawled out from the bottom of the pile of toys. "You won't catch me now – and you won't get this back, either!" And, with that, he waved the cat with the magic Emerald eye at the girls, stuck his tongue out and ran off!

After that Goblin!

"After him!" Emily cried anxiously. "He's still got my Emerald!"

Rachel and Kirsty chased after the goblin, with Emily flying alongside. Luckily, there weren't any customers about to see what was going on. But the goblin was very cunning. He dodged here and there, disappearing

behind displays, and always managing
to keep one step ahead of the girls.

"Maybe if we split up, we'd have
a better chance of catching him,"
Rachel panted.

Kirsty slowed and looked around.
"Where's he gone now?" she asked.
The goblin was nowhere to be seen.

"He was here a minute ago,"
Rachel said, puzzled. "He can't have
just disappeared."

"There he is!" Emily shouted, pointing with her sparkly wand.

The girls turned and saw the goblin running towards the stairs as fast as he could go, the toy cat bobbing up and down in his arms.

"Don't let him get away!" Rachel gasped, hurtling after the fleeing goblin.

The sound of footsteps coming up the stairs made the goblin skid to a halt.

Realising the stairs were blocked, he looked around frantically for another means of escape. Then he plunged behind some shelves stacked with toy cars and trucks.

The girls and Emily followed, racing down one aisle just in time to see the goblin turn the corner into the next.

"I think we're catching him," said
Kirsty. "Keep going!"

Rachel and Kirsty
dashed round the
corner, and almost
tripped over.

The goblin was
pulling boxes of
toys off the shelves,
and throwing them
in the girls' path.

"Wait a moment, girls!" Emily
called, as the goblin raced off again,
cackling with glee. With an expert
wave of her wand, she scattered fairy
dust over the boxes. Immediately,
they floated up into the air and
neatly stacked themselves back
on the shelves.

"Why don't we split up?" Rachel whispered to Kirsty and Emily in a low voice. "Then we might be able to trap him."

"Good idea," Kirsty agreed.

At the end of the aisle, Kirsty and Emily went left, and Rachel went right. The goblin had disappeared again. But as Rachel ran between the shelves of toys, she saw him dash across the bottom of the aisle, right in front of her.

"Got you!" she panted, reaching out to grab him by the shoulder.

But the goblin was too quick for her. He snatched a blue skateboard from a nearby shelf, flung it to the floor and jumped on board. Rachel's fingers clutched at thin air as the goblin sailed off across the polished floor.

"You nearly had him, Rachel!" Emily shouted encouragingly, whizzing over to her.

"Look," Kirsty gasped, rushing to join her friends, "he's heading for the lift!"

The doors of the lift stood open, waiting for passengers, and the skateboard was zooming straight towards them. The goblin glanced back at the girls with a smug smile, waving the toy cat triumphantly.

"Oh, no, we'll never catch him now!" wailed Emily.

But Kirsty wasn't going to give up yet. She looked at the toys on the shelves around her, searching for something, anything, that might stop the goblin. Her gaze fell on a stack of brightly-painted boomerangs.

"Emily, can you use your magic to help me?" she asked, grabbing one from the top of the pile.

Emily nodded and lifted her wand. Kirsty aimed the boomerang at the toy cat in the goblin's hand, and threw it. The boomerang whistled through the air, but as it got nearer to the goblin, it started to

drift a little off course. Rachel bit her lip in alarm, it looked as though the goblin was going to get away with the Emerald in spite of all their efforts.

But Emily waved her wand, and a cloud of sparkling fairy dust shot after the boomerang. As soon as the fairy magic touched the toy, the boomerang swerved back on course and flew straight towards the goblin like an arrow.

The friends watched as the
boomerang spun through the air,
struck the toy cat, and knocked it right
out of the goblin's hand! The black cat
fell to the floor, but the skateboard kept
on going. The goblin let out a howl
of annoyance.

Going Up

"Pesky fairy magic!" the goblin shouted angrily. But there was nothing he could do. The skateboard was zooming along too fast for him to jump off. He glanced over his shoulder just as Kirsty and Rachel dashed forwards and picked up the toy cat.

"Give that back!" yelled the goblin,

as the skateboard
zoomed on
towards the lift.
"You must
be joking!"
Rachel laughed.
"Hadn't you better
look where you're
going?" called Kirsty.

The skateboard whizzed through the

open doors of the
lift and crashed
into the back wall,
depositing the
goblin in a heap
on the floor. He
staggered to his feet,

unhurt, but looking very cross indeed.

Furiously, he made a rush towards the doors, but they slammed shut, trapping him inside. Ting! The lift began to move upwards.

"Goodbye, goblin," Emily called.

Kirsty and Rachel laughed as they heard a muffled roar of rage from inside the lift.

"Girls, you've done it again," Emily declared, fluttering down to sit on Kirsty's shoulder. "How can I ever thank you?"

"We're just glad we got your Emerald back," replied Kirsty, holding up the black cat. The beautiful magic Emerald winked and sparkled at them.

"Sorry, Kitty," Emily said, smiling at the toy cat, "but I need my Emerald more than you do!" She raised her wand and a shower of green sparkles floated down over the black cat. The magic Emerald fell gently into Kirsty's hand, and a new green eye appeared in its place.

"And now it's back to Fairyland for you," Emily added, touching her wand to the jewel. "Queen Titania and King Oberon will be very pleased to see you!"

A fountain of sparkling green fairy dust shot up from the jewel, and then the Emerald vanished from Kirsty's hand.

"Rachel, we'd better go down and meet your dad," Kirsty said, looking at her watch.

"Yes, and I think we'll use the stairs!" Rachel agreed, laughing.

"Thank you for your help, girls," Emily said in her pretty, silvery voice. "Every jewel you find takes us one step closer to restoring the jewels' magic to Fairyland."

She waved her wand. "Goodbye and good luck!" And she disappeared in a flash of fairy dust.

Rachel and Kirsty grinned at each other and then hurried downstairs.

Rachel's dad was waiting by the shop entrance, with lots of carrier bags. "Ah, there you are, girls," he said with a grin. "Will you give me a hand with these?" He handed them each a carrier bag.

"Lucky old Mark!" said Rachel, taking a peep inside. "He's going to get lots of presents for his birthday."

Her dad looked a bit embarrassed. "Well, some of these things are for me, actually," he said. "I'm thinking of putting a toy train track in the attic."

Rachel laughed. "That sounds like a great idea, Dad."

"That was quite an adventure!" Kirsty whispered to Rachel as they followed Mr Walker out of the shop.

Rachel nodded. Then she grinned and gestured towards her dad, who was marching happily along the street with his bags, eagerly explaining his plans for the attic. "From the sound of it, our next adventure is going to involve fewer fairies and more trains!" she said, laughing.

**Now Rachel and Kirsty
must help...**

Chloe the Topaz Fairy

Read on for a sneak peek...

"There's a fancy dress shop!"
Kirsty Tate said, pointing at one
of the shops on Cherrywell's busy
high street.

"Brilliant!" Rachel Walker replied
happily. "Let's go and choose
costumes for Isabel's Halloween
party before the bus arrives."

"OK," Kirsty agreed. She was
staying at Rachel's house for half-
term week and the girls had just been
bowling with some of Rachel's friends
from school. One of them, Isabel,

had invited everyone to a Halloween party at the weekend. "What do you want to dress up as?" Kirsty asked Rachel.

"Something magical, of course!" Rachel replied with a grin.

Kirsty smiled back. She and Rachel loved magic.

It was because they shared an amazing secret: they were friends with the fairies!

Their magical adventures had started one summer when the girls had helped the fairies stop Jack Frost from taking the colour away from Fairyland. Since then, the Fairy King and Queen had asked for their help several times.

In fact, that very week, Rachel and Kirsty were right in the middle of another fairy adventure, because Jack

Frost was causing trouble again!

This time he'd stolen seven sparkling jewels from Queen Titania's tiara. The jewels were very precious because they controlled special fairy powers, like the fairies' ability to fly, or to give children in the human world sweet dreams. Every year, in a special celebration, the fairies would recharge their wands with the jewels' magic. This year's ceremony was due to take place in just a few days' time. If the gems weren't found by then, the fairies would run out of the jewels' special magic completely!

Jack Frost had hoped to keep the magic jewels himself. But when their magical light had started to melt his ice castle, he had flown into a rage and cast a spell to hurl the gems into the human world. Then he sent his mean goblin servants to guard them so that the fairies couldn't get them back.

Rachel and Kirsty had already helped three of the Jewel Fairies recover their magic gems, but there were still four jewels left to find.

"Do you think we'll find another jewel today?" Rachel whispered as she and Kirsty ran up to the shop.

"I hope so," Kirsty replied...

Read Chloe the Topaz Fairy to find out what adventures are in store for Kirsty and Rachel!

Calling all parents, carers and teachers!
The Rainbow Magic fairies are here to help
your child enter the magical world of reading.
Whatever reading stage they are at, there's
a Rainbow Magic book for everyone!
Here is Lydia the Reading Fairy's guide to
supporting your child's journey at all levels.

Starting Out

1 Our Rainbow Magic Beginner Readers are perfect for first-time readers who are just beginning to develop reading skills and confidence. Approved by teachers, they contain a full range of educational levelling, as well as lively full-colour illustrations.

Developing Readers

2 Rainbow Magic Early Readers contain longer stories and wider vocabulary for building stamina and growing confidence. These are adaptations of our most popular Rainbow Magic stories, specially developed for younger readers in conjunction with an Early Years reading consultant, with full-colour illustrations.

Going Solo

3 The Rainbow Magic chapter books – a mixture of series and one-off specials – contain accessible writing to encourage your child to venture into reading independently. These highly collectible and much-loved magical stories inspire a love of reading to last a lifetime.

www.rainbowmagicbooks.co.uk

"Rainbow Magic got my daughter reading chapter books. Great sparkly covers, cute fairies and traditional stories full of magic that she found impossible to put down" – Mother of Edie (6 years)

"Florence LOVES the Rainbow Magic books. She really enjoys reading now" Mother of Florence (6 years)

Read along the Reading Rainbow!

Well done – you have completed the book!

This book was worth 1 star.

See how far you have climbed on the Reading Rainbow.
The more books you read, the more stars you can colour in
and the closer you will be to becoming a Royal Fairy!

Do you want to print your own Reading Rainbow?

1) Go to the Rainbow Magic website

2) Download and print out the poster

3) Colour in a star for every book you finish
and climb the Reading Rainbow

4) For every step up the rainbow,
you can download your very own certificate

There's all this and lots more at
rainbowmagicbooks.co.uk

You'll find activities, stories, a special newsletter
AND you can search for the fairy with your name!